READING RAINBOW® READERS

SCARY STORIES

to Read When It's Dark

SeaStar Books

NEW YORK

Special thanks to Leigh Ann Jones, Valerie Lewis, Walter Mayes, and Marian Reiner for the consultation services and invaluable support they provided for the creation of this book.

Reading Rainbow® is a production of GPN/Nebraska ETV and WNED-TV Buffalo and is produced by Lancit Media Entertainment, Ltd., a JuniorNet Company. Reading Rainbow® is a registered trademark of GPN/WNED-TV.

Collection copyright © 2000 by SeaStar Books, a division of North-South Books, Inc. *The following are gratefully acknowledged for granting permission to reprint the material in this book:* "Shivers" from *Days with Frog and Toad.* Copyright © 1979 by Arnold Lobel. Used by permission of HarperCollins Publishers. • "The Green Ribbon" from *In a Dark, Dark, Room.* Text copyright © 1984 by Alvin Schwartz. Illustrations copyright © 1984 by Dirk Zimmer. Used by permission of HarperCollins Publishers. • "Halloween" from *EEK! Stories to Make You Shriek!* by Jane O'Connor, illustrations by Brian Karas. Text copyright © 1992 by Jane O'Connor. Illustrations copyright © 1992 by G. Brian Karas. Used by permission of Grosset & Dunlap, Inc., a division of Penguin Putnam Inc. • "Henry's Bedtime Story" from *The Happy Hocky Family* by Lane Smith. Copyright © 1993 by Lane Smith. Used by permission of Viking Penguin, a division of Penguin Putnam Inc. • "The Dark Wood" from *BOO! Stories to Make You Jump,* compiled by Laura Cecil, illustrated by Emma Chichester Clark. Illustrations copyright © 1990 by Emma Chichester Clark. Used by permission of the compiler and the artist. • "Bloody Fingers" from *Five Funny Frights* by Judith Bauer Stamper, illustrated by Tim Raglin. Text copyright © 1993 by Judith Bauer Stamper. Illustrations copyright © 1993 by Tim Raglin. Used by permission of Scholastic Inc. • "Something at the Window" from *Ant Plays Bear* by Betsy Byars. Text copyright © 1997 by Betsy Byars. Illustrations copyright © 1997 by Marc Simont. Used by permission of Viking Penguin, a division of Penguin Putnam Inc.

SeaStar Books · A division of North-South Books, Inc.

ISBN 1-58717-036-1 (library binding) 10 9 8 7 6 5 4 3 2 1
ISBN 1-58717-035-3 (paperback) 10 9 8 7 6 5 4 3 2 1

Contents

Shivers

BY Arnold Lobel

The night was cold and dark.
"Listen to the wind
howling in the trees," said Frog.
"What a fine time for a ghost story."
Toad moved deeper into his chair.
"Toad," asked Frog,
"don't you like to be scared?
Don't you like to feel the shivers?"
"I am not too sure," said Toad

Frog made a fresh pot of tea.
He sat down
and began a story.

"When I was small," said Frog,
"my mother and father and I
went out for a picnic.
On the way home we lost our way.
My mother was worried.
'We must get home,' she said.
'We do not want to meet
the Old Dark Frog.'
'Who is that?' I asked.

'A terrible ghost,'
said my father.
'He comes out at night and eats
little frog children for supper.'"
Toad sipped his tea.

"Frog," he asked,
"are you making this up?"
"Maybe yes and maybe no,"
said Frog.

"My mother and father
went to search for a path,"
said Frog.
"They told me to wait
until they came back.
I sat under a tree and waited.
The woods became dark.
I was afraid.
Then I saw two huge eyes.
It was the Old Dark Frog.

"He was standing near me."

"Frog," asked Toad,
"did this really happen?"
"Maybe it did
and maybe it didn't,"
said Frog.

Frog went on with the story.
"The Dark Frog pulled
a jump rope out of his pocket.

'I am not hungry now,'
said the Dark Frog.
'I have eaten too many
tasty frog children.
But after I jump rope
one hundred times,
I will be hungry again.
Then I will eat YOU!'"

"The Dark Frog tied one end
of the rope to a tree.
'Turn for me!' he shouted.
I turned the rope for the Dark Frog.
He jumped twenty times.
'I am beginning to get hungry,'
said the Dark Frog.

He jumped fifty times.
'I am getting hungrier,'
said the Dark Frog.
He jumped ninety times.
'I am very hungry now!'
said the Dark Frog."

"What happened then?"
asked Toad.
"I had to save my life,"
said Frog.
"I ran around
and around the tree
with the rope.
I tied up
the Old Dark Frog.
He roared and screamed.

"I ran away fast."

"I found my mother and father,"
said Frog.
"We came safely home."

"Frog," asked Toad,
"was that a true story?"
"Maybe it was
and maybe it wasn't,"
said Frog.

Frog and Toad sat
close by the fire.
They were scared.
The teacups shook
in their hands.
They were having the shivers.
It was a good, warm feeling.

The Green Ribbon

RETOLD BY **Alvin Schwartz**
PICTURES BY **Dirk Zimmer**

Once there was a girl named Jenny.
She was like all the other girls,
except for one thing.
She always wore a green ribbon
around her neck.

There was a boy named Alfred
in her class.
Alfred liked Jenny,
and Jenny liked Alfred.

One day he asked her,
"Why do you wear that ribbon
all the time?"
"I cannot tell you," said Jenny.
But Alfred kept asking,
"Why *do* you wear it?"
And Jenny would say,
"It is not important."

Jenny and Alfred grew up
and fell in love.
One day they got married.

After their wedding,
Alfred said,
"Now that we are married,
you must tell me
about the green ribbon."
"You still must wait,"
said Jenny.
"I will tell you
when the right time comes."

Years passed.

Alfred and Jenny grew old.

One day Jenny became very sick.

The doctor told her
she was dying.
Jenny called Alfred to her side.

"Alfred," she said,
"now I can tell you
about the green ribbon.
Untie it,
and you will see
why I could not tell you before."
Slowly and carefully,
Alfred untied the ribbon,

and Jenny's head fell off.

Halloween

BY Jane O'Connor
PICTURES BY G. Brian Karas

It was Halloween.

Ted was waiting for his friend Danny.

They were going to a party.

Ted already had on his costume.
He wore white pants,
a white shirt,
a black belt,
and a black headband.
He was a karate guy.

"Be sure to wear a coat,"
Ted's mother called.
Ted made a face.
"Come on, Ma.
Karate guys do not wear coats."
Ted's mother did not care.
"It is cold out.
You wear a coat.
Or you cannot go to the party."
Ted made another face.
But he put on his coat.
Then he went to wait for Danny.

It was dark now.
The trees made spooky shadows
on the street.
Ted hoped Danny would come soon.
Then he saw Danny
coming down the street.

Danny was dressed as a monster.
He wore a furry brown suit
with furry paws and claws.
Over his head was a monster mask.
"Wow! Cool costume," said Ted.
"Gronk," was all Danny said.
Then off they went to the party.

The party was fun.

Everyone bobbed for apples

and ate pizza for dinner.

There was a costume contest.
Danny won.
"Gronk!" said Danny,
when he got the prize.
It was a big bag of candy.

On the way home
Danny ate all his candy.
He let out a big burp.

"Gross!" said Ted.

"Gronk!" said Danny.

Then Ted waved good-bye.

The next day Ted went
to Danny's house.
They always walked to school together.
Danny's mother opened the door.
"Danny is sick," she said.
"He cannot go to school today."
Ted felt bad.
"I bet it was all the junk
Danny ate at the party," said Ted.
Danny's mother looked puzzled.
"The party?
Danny did not go to the party.
He was sick in bed all night,"
said Danny's mother.

Then *who* was the monster at the party?

Henry's Bedtime Story

BY Lane Smith

"Holly,
do you know the story
of the
MONSTER
who comes to
STEAL
little children
in the night?

"He comes into kids' bedrooms
at twelve midnight.

Big MONSTER.
Scary MONSTER.
Bad MONSTER."

"I will lock the door after you leave,"
said Holly.
"You don't have to worry about that,
silly, . . .

. . . the Monster only comes in
through windows."

The Dark Wood

TRADITIONAL

PICTURES BY Emma Chichester Clark

In the dark, dark wood
Was a dark, dark house,

In the dark, dark house
Was a dark, dark room,

In the dark, dark room
Was a dark, dark cupboard,

In the dark, dark cupboard
Was a dark, dark shelf,

And on the dark, dark shelf
Was a dark, dark box,

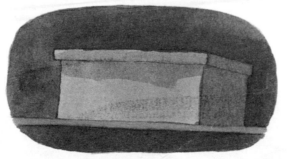

And in that dark, dark box

Was

a

GHOST!

Bloody Fingers

BY Judith Bauer Stamper
PICTURES BY Tim Raglin

Two brothers were camping out
in the woods.
They had gone on a long walk
through the tall, dark trees.
Now they were lost.

The sun was sinking lower and
lower in the sky.
"I think camp is that way," one said.
"I think it's the other way,"
the second said.
They stood looking at each other,
not knowing what to do.

Both of them were really scared.
Just then, they heard a sound
behind them.
Something was coming toward them
through the woods.
They turned around and looked.

It was a man, coming closer
and closer.
He was holding his hands
up in the air.
"Bloody fingers!" he called out
in a scary voice.

The two brothers looked at each
other with wide eyes.
Then they started to run.
The man ran after them.
"Bloody fingers!" he screamed.

The brothers ran faster and faster.
But the man kept up with them.
He held out his fingers.
They could see the blood!

"Bloody fingers!"
the man kept calling.
The boys were shaking
with fear now.
Then they saw their camp.
Maybe they could make it
to their tent!

The boys ran into the campground.
But the man kept right on
running after them.
"Bloody fingers!" he yelled.
He was getting closer and closer.

Just in time, the brothers ran into
their tent and hid under their cots.
Their mother and father were gone.
But their little sister was there.
Outside the tent, the man was still
screaming, "Bloody fingers!"

The little sister looked at her brothers
hiding under the cots.
Then she peeked through the tent
flap to look at the man.
"Bloody fingers!" he screamed
at her.

The girl picked up something
from a box in the tent.
Then she walked outside.
The man pointed his bloody fingers
at her.

"Bloody fingers!" he yelled.

"HAVE A BAND-AID!" she said.

Something at the Window

BY Betsy Byars

PICTURES BY Marc Simont

Tap tap.

"There is someone tapping
on our window," Ant said.

"Ant, I am trying to get to sleep."

"Me, too, but I can't.

Someone is tapping on the window."

I said, "Ant, be real.

Our room is on the second floor.

No one could tap on our window."

"A giant could," Ant said.

"There are no giants," I said.

"Well, someone with very long legs."
"Everyone with very long legs
is playing basketball.
Now, Ant, go to sleep," I said.
"Will you look?" Ant asked.
"What?"
"Will you pull back the curtain and look?"
"Then will you go to sleep?" I said.

"Yes," said Ant.

I went to the window.

I pulled back the curtain.

"There is nobody there," I said.

"Then what is going *tap tap*
like that?"

"The tree. The tree!" I said.

"The wind is blowing.

A branch of the tree is tapping
at the window."

I got back into bed.

"Good night, Ant."

"See, I was right," Ant said.

"There was somebody
tapping on the window."

"A tree! A tree!" I said.

"A tree is not somebody!

"Now this is the last time
I'm saying this.
Good night, Ant!"
"Good night."
Then Ant said softly,
"Good night, tree."
Tap tap.